MILO ON WHEELS

Elizabeth Gordon

An imprint of Enslow Publishing

WEST **44** BOOKS™

the CLUB

Milo on Wheels

Javi Takes a Bow

Addy's Big Splash

Noah the Con Artist

Club Zoe

Please visit our website, www.west44books.com. For a free color catalog of all our high-quality books, call toll free 1-800-542-2595 or fax 1-877-542-2596.

Cataloging-in-Publication Data

Names: Gordon, Elizabeth.
Title: Milo on wheels / Elizabeth Gordon.
Description: New York : West 44, 2019. | Series: The club
Identifiers: ISBN 9781538382370 (pbk.) | ISBN 9781538382387 (library bound) | ISBN 9781538383193 (ebook)
Subjects: LCSH: Friendship--Juvenile fiction. | Karting--Juvenile fiction. | After-school programs--Juvenile fiction. | People with disabilities--Juvenile fiction.
Classification: LCC PZ7.G673 Mi 2019 | DDC [E]--dc23

First Edition

Published in 2019 by
Enslow Publishing
111 East 14th Street, Suite 349
New York, NY 10003

Editor: Theresa Emminizer
Designer: Sam DeMartin

Photo Credits: front matter (basketball) LHF Graphics/Shutterstock.com; front matter (planets) Nikolaeva/Shutterstock.com; front matter (hurricane) GO BANANAS DESIGN STUDIO/Shutterstock.com; front matter (stickers) U.Pimages_vector/Shutterstock.com; front matter (paint splatter) Milan M/Shutterstock.com; front matter (boomerang) hchjjl/Shutterstock.com; front matter (game strategy) Dejan Popovic/Shutterstock.com; front matter (broken bone) BlueRingMedia/Shutterstock.com; front matter (Guatemala stamp) astudio/Shutterstock.com; front matter (bandaids) lineartestpilot/Shutterstock.com; front matter (ants) Viktorija Reuta/Shutterstock.com; front matter (billboard) Franzi/Shutterstock.com; p. 2 olllikeballoon/Shutterstock.com; p. 5 Aluna1/Shutterstock.com; p. 9 nikiteev_konstantin/Shutterstock.com; p. 11 AlexHliv/Shutterstock.com; p. 17 Pramega/Shutterstock.com; p. 19 (dandelion) Kudryashka/Shutterstock.com; p. 19 (pill bug) bsd/Shutterstock.com; pp. 22, 45, 54 LHF Graphics/Shutterstock.com; p. 24 owatta/Shutterstock.com; p. 26 ArtMari/Shutterstock.com; p. 32 Yoonki/Shutterstock.com; p. 35 John T Takai/Shutterstock.com; p. 40 predragilevski/Shutterstock.com; pp. 53 (helmet), 56 (wheel), 57 (flags), 59 (wheel) Fafarumba/Shutterstock.com; p. 55 Dmitry Natashin/Shutterstock.com; p. 59 (bolt) Aleks Melnik/Shutterstock.com; p. 63 Nikolaeva/Shutterstock.com; back matter (music notes) mhatzapa/Shutterstock.com; back matter (headphones) sintopic/Shutterstock.com.

Printed in the United States of America

CPSIA compliance information: Batch #CS18W44: For further information contact Enslow Publishing, LLC, New York, New York at 1-800-542-2595.

the CLUB

Milo Braverman

Most likely to have a toad in his pocket

COMEBACK KID

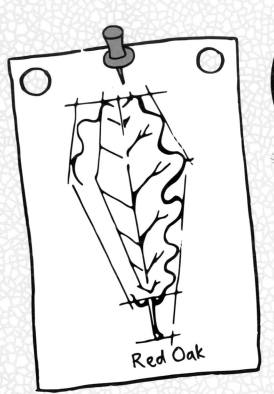

Red Oak

EMBODIMENT OF TEVYE

Javi Morales

Most likely to know all the words to Hamilton

Addy Prescott

Most likely to break an arm playing ping-pong

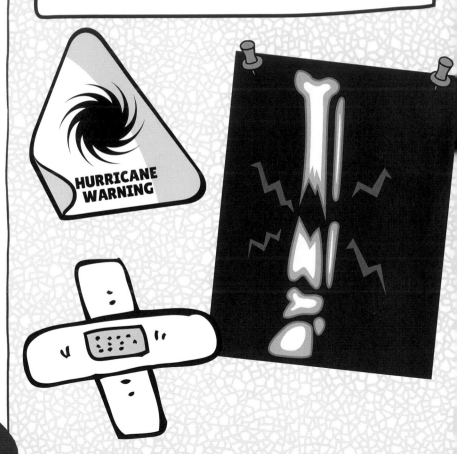

Noah Spencer

Most likely to have paint in his hair

RESIDENT ARTIST

Zoe Spencer

Most likely to correct your free throw form

PLAYER OF THE GAME

Chapter One
The Club

Milo stared out the car window. A sign read Parkside Community Center. Behind it was a big brick building standing on the edge of a large city park. It looked a little old and run down. But also cheerful and clean. He could see artwork hanging in most of the windows. He noticed how many kids were hanging around. There was a noisy group right by the front doors. He felt a knot in the pit of his stomach.

There are lots of steps, Milo thought hopefully. *Maybe I won't be able to get in.* Stairs were hard for him.

His door opened. Milo's mom handed him his crutches. She picked up his backpack. "Okay, Sport, let's go. There's a smaller staircase around the side of the building."

Milo sighed. He'd have to go in. Worse, he'd

have to pass all those kids to get to the other stairs. So much for staying unnoticed.

He stood up. Slid his arms into his crutches. Forced his unwilling leg muscles to move. The crutches squeaked as he wobbled forward. Milo had overheard a teacher talking about him once. She said he walked like a drunken sailor. It was true. His twisted legs never did quite what he wanted them to. Even with braces, they jerked in odd directions. Milo could hear whispering. He was sure it was about him.

Milo made his way up the stairs. A tall man with big, tattooed arms was standing inside the door.

"Hi, Milo," he said. "I'm Miguel. I'm the director of Parkside's after-school program. We call it The Club. Let me show you around."

Milo and his mom followed Miguel around the building. The inside looked like the outside. Old, but bright and well-kept. There were posters, announcements, and art projects all over the walls. He had to admit that The Club was pretty cool. There was a pool, an art room, a gym, an auditorium, a tutoring center, and a snack area.

"I've been running The Club for about ten years," Miguel said to Milo's mom. "We want kids to feel comfortable here. Like it's a second home. And we want to encourage them to try lots of different things."

There certainly were kids *everywhere*. And they were doing all sorts of things. Miguel kept stopping to talk to them. He knew everyone's name. He asked about their days or what they were working on. He reminded them about rules or helped them with their homework. He knew if kids were where they were supposed to be or not. He seemed strict, but kind.

Milo found the busy, crowded spaces a bit overwhelming. He tried to hide behind Miguel each time they walked into a new room. It was no use. Kids turned their heads towards him. They were staring at his legs and crutches. It was hard not to attract attention.

Miguel noticed how uncomfortable Milo was. He said, "Your mom told me you want to be a biologist. She said you're making a field guide of all the plants and animals you find. Let me show you what we have outdoors. There's a reason our building is called Parkside."

He led Milo and his mom out a back door. This was definitely better. There were lots of kids playing on the playground and basketball court. There were also picnic tables tucked into

quiet corners. And there were so many trees! The September sun shone though their leaves. It made patterns on the ground. The community center's backyard opened right into the park.

Milo had moved with his mom and dad into the city two years ago. The park reminded him of the woods behind his old house. He missed the green and the quiet.

His mom turned to him. She smiled, but she looked worried. "What do you think?"

Milo thought about his last after-school program.

He remembered the whispers.

He remembered kids joking about the way he walked.

He remembered being tripped. That hadn't been an accident, no matter what people had said. Milo's parents had pulled him out of the old program. He knew how much his parents wanted him to like this new place. He had to go somewhere after school until his parents could pick him up. Miguel was nice. The Club was big. There were places to disappear. He could sit at a table under one of the trees. Work on his field guide. He took a deep breath.

"Okay," Milo said. "I'll try it."

Chapter Two
Milo's Plan

The next day the bus dropped Milo off at The Club. Two hours until his mom came to pick him up. He didn't want to be teased. He didn't want anyone to feel sorry for him. He wanted to be left alone.

Milo made his way through the halls. He could feel his nervousness rising. He took up so much room with his crutches. Kids were moving out of his way. They were staring at him. But Milo had a plan.

Milo went out the back door. He went past a bunch of basketball players. He went past the playground full of screaming, laughing kids. He didn't look up. He didn't look around. He didn't want anyone to talk to him. He headed straight for a big tree. There were two picnic tables under it. There was a boy wearing headphones sitting at one. He was about Milo's age. The other table was empty.

Milo sat down. He tucked his crutches out of sight. Then he pulled out a sketchbook labeled "Field Guide." He found his box of drawing pencils and his books. He plucked a leaf from a nearby branch and started to

Field Guide

work. Being busy was part of his plan.

Miguel stopped by. "There you are, Milo," he said. "I wanted to see if you'd like to sign up for any activities. There are art classes. There are swimming lessons. There's a chess club…"

"Thanks," Milo said. "But I'm not really interested. I've got my own project."

Miguel glanced down at the guide. "That's pretty cool. But won't it be a bit lonely if it's the only thing you do?" Milo shrugged. *That's what I want*, he thought. *To be left alone.*

Miguel smiled and said, "You don't have to make up your mind right away. Take a few days to get to know the place. Let me know if there is anything I can help you with."

He left. Milo opened his tree identification book. He studied his leaf. It matched the picture of a red oak leaf. He was pleased. That was a new one for his field guide. He found a blank page and wrote "Red Oak." He started to draw the leaf.

His nervousness faded as he focused on his task. The sun was warm. The shade was cool. There was a gentle breeze blowing. A family of squirrels was chasing itself in the branches over his head. He could almost imagine he was in his old backyard, away from all the concrete of the city.

Red Oak

But then Miguel showed up again. This time there were a couple of kids with him. They were carrying drinks and pretzel bags.

"I wanted you to meet some other members of The Club," said Miguel. "This is Noah." A boy with short, spiky dreadlocks said, "Hey, man." Miguel glanced at Milo's guide. "Noah is The

Club's resident artist. Maybe you two can talk about drawing."

Milo shut his book. Miguel ignored this and said, "And this is Addy." A tall, red-haired girl smiled and tried to wave. The drinks she had been carrying fell to the ground. Noah laughed and helped her pick up the cans, saying, "Hurricane Addy strikes again!"

Miguel gave him a *that's enough* kind of look. He said, "Addy has been coming to The Club for a long time. She can introduce you to everyone and answer any questions."

Miguel walked away. He was always on the move. Noah and Addy sat down at the table. They offered Milo a drink and a bag of pretzels. He took them and mumbled, "Thanks." Noah asked him if he liked art. Addy asked him where he went to school. He answered all their questions as briefly as possible. He was sure they didn't want to be there.

They were being nice to him because Miguel had told them to.

Soon, the snacks were gone. Milo hoped they would leave. Noah had run out of questions. But Addy was trying to keep the conversation going. She was very chatty. "There are lots of special events," she said. "There's the winter musical, the art show, the spring carnival, the end-of-the-year dance, a basketball tournament…"

"Yeah," said Noah. "My sister Zoe is the captain of our basketball team. And there's a go-kart rally at the end of this month. It's so cool! We build go-karts and race them down a hill in the park."

Milo frowned. *Dancing? Basketball? Go-kart races? Do they see my legs? Are they making fun of me?* Milo wanted this conversation to end. He shoved his things into his backpack and grabbed his crutches. "Thanks for the snack," he said. He stood up. "I think my ride is here." He turned and went back into the building.

Milo found a chair in a far corner of the tutoring center and sat down. He checked the clock. *An hour and a half to go*, he thought. *Maybe my plan will work better tomorrow*.

Chapter Three
Javi

The next day was better. There was an empty picnic table under the red oak. The only other person nearby was the boy with the headphones. He glanced up when Milo went past, but he didn't say anything. It seemed like he wanted to be left alone, too.

Milo sat down. He took his things out of his backpack. He spread them over the table. He wanted it to look full. He opened his field guide and started to work on his new entry.

Once, out of the corner of his eye, he thought he saw Addy and Noah. They were standing with a group of kids nearby. Would they try to talk to him? He turned his body away. He bent over his work. They didn't come over.

Miguel stopped to ask how he was doing. "Fine," Milo answered. He smiled. He tried to look relaxed. Milo wanted everyone to get the message. The Club was a place for him to wait for his parents. Nothing more. He wasn't interested in being a part of anything. He wasn't going to give anyone a chance to laugh at him or pity him. Miguel left. He hadn't mentioned any activities. Milo's plan was working.

For the next few days, Milo stayed out of the way. The weather was beautiful. He could wander around the edges of the yard. Search for new plants and bugs. He could pull out his binoculars and watch the birds up in the trees. And he could

sit at the picnic table and work on his guide. He found lots of new entries for it. But his favorite new page was still the one with the red oak.

There were lots of these trees all over the park. But the one he was sitting under was special. There was an old iron fence running along the edge of the yard. The oak had actually grown around and through it. In some places, it had wrapped itself around the bars. It looked like it was swallowing them.

Milo thought about the tiny acorn that had fallen between the railings 70 or 80 years ago. It was a hard place to grow. Hard, but not impossible. The acorn had sprouted. The seedling had overcome everything standing in its way. It had found its bit of sunlight. Now it was a huge tree. Milo knew that plants did not have feelings. Still, he kept thinking that the tree was brave.

When Milo got into the car on Friday, his mom asked, "How did your day go?"

"Great," Milo answered right away. *And I kind of mean it*, Milo thought. His guide was coming along nicely. People were leaving him alone. Just like he wanted. Sure, he caught himself watching other kids. They were chatting and running around. He watched Noah and Addy. But that's what scientists do, he thought. They observe.

In fact, Milo had often observed the boy with the headphones. This was easy to do without drawing attention. The boy was usually focusing on his work. He always sat at the same table. Just like Milo. He was thin. Long, dark bangs flopped over his eyes. Milo noticed that the boy wore the same thing nearly every day. The clothes were neat and clean, but they were faded and worn. When Miguel came by, he spoke to him in Spanish. Once, Milo saw the boy pull his music player out of his pocket. It was a battered portable cassette player. He couldn't believe the boy was using something so old. He was surprised that it worked. Milo wondered what his story was.

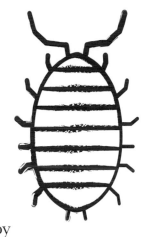

Soon, Milo discovered he wasn't the only one who could observe things. Early the following week, Milo found a pill bug. It had been hiding under a rock near the basketball court. Milo was trying to draw it. It was tricky, because it kept crawling away. Suddenly, he realized the boy with the headphones was standing across from him. He looked up. The boy laid a yellow flower down on the field guide.

"You draw this?" the boy said. He spoke slowly, as if the words were hard to pronounce.

"It's a dandelion," Milo said.

The boy nodded. "Pretty," he said. He flung out his arm. "Everywhere."

Milo laughed. "Yeah," he said. "I guess it is."

"Javi," the boy said, pointing to himself.

"Milo," Milo answered.

Javi looked down. The pill bug was trying to escape again. He pulled a small, clear box out of his pocket. It was a case for a cassette tape. Javi scooped up the pill bug. He put it in the box and shut it. "Ha!" Javi said. He smiled and handed Milo the box.

Milo smiled back.

"Thanks," he said. Javi kept standing there.

Milo hesitated. Then he pushed his books to one side of the table. He pointed to the empty space.

"Do you want to sit down?"

Chapter Four
The Hurricane

From that day on, Milo and Javi shared a table. If it was sunny, they sat outside. If it was rainy, they sat in the snack area. They didn't say much. Javi didn't speak a lot of English. Milo could learn only two things about him. One was that he had moved from Guatemala last summer. The other was that he loved old musicals. His backpack was full of cassette tapes.

They were all recordings of Broadway shows.

Javi sometimes brought Milo new things to draw. Milo sometimes helped Javi with his homework. Mostly they sat quietly, each doing their own thing. *But*, Milo thought, *it's nice to have someone else doing their own thing next to you.*

Milo could tell Miguel was happy that he and Javi were sitting together. He didn't mention it though. He *did* keep mentioning Club activities. The go-kart rally was starting soon. He wanted Milo and Javi to sign up for it. "It's not too late," Miguel said. "Every kid who's in middle school can join a team. Each team builds its own wooden kart. There are lots of ways to participate —design, construction, painting…"

Javi looked worried. Milo knew he didn't like speaking in front of most people. He'd hate being on a team. Milo wouldn't care for it much either. He'd seen that type of go-kart before. You steered it with your legs like an old wooden sled. Milo couldn't control his legs very well. They would often move when he didn't want them to. There was no way he could use them to steer. It didn't sound fun to build something he couldn't use.

"No, thanks," Milo said. "We're kind of busy." Javi nodded. They were going to stay in their quiet corner.

At least, that's what they thought. The next day Milo and Javi had settled down at their table when they saw Addy coming toward them. She wasn't carrying snacks this time. She was walking on crutches.

"Hi, Milo," Addy said. She lowered herself onto a bench. "Looks like I'll be joining you for a while."

Javi pulled off his headphones. Milo stared at her blankly. There was an empty table right beside them. She hadn't even asked to sit down.

Addy didn't seem to notice their surprise. She kept talking. "I tripped over my backpack," she said, pointing at her leg. "That wouldn't have mattered if I hadn't also fallen down the stairs. Spiral fracture of the tibia. Six to eight weeks." She sighed. "Hurricane Addy strikes again, right?"

Javi was confused. He turned to Milo. "Hurricane?"

Addy grimaced. "Yeah. That's what people call me. Like a storm. A natural disaster. Let's just say this isn't my first broken bone." She tilted her head. "You're Javi, right? Miguel thought I could help you with your English. I signed up to work for the tutoring center. I can't do much else right now." Milo and Javi looked at each other. Addy took this as agreement.

"Great!" she said. She turned to Milo. "You won't mind us working here, will you? The weather's so nice. It would be a shame to be inside."

Milo nodded. What else could he do? He felt a bit caught in a storm himself. Maybe more of a tornado of emotions than a hurricane. "Besides," Addy continued. "Soon everyone will be outside working on their go-karts. The rally is next week. I'm so bummed I broke my leg. But at least we can watch."

Addy turned to Javi. She started checking over his homework. Javi was embarrassed, but Milo began to relax. Maybe he could get some work done now. He opened his guide to the "dandelion" page. His drawing was coming along nicely. It only needed a little shading along the left side…

"Whoa!" Addy's voice broke in on his thoughts. Before he could stop her, she had picked up the guide. "Is this what you're always working on over here? I was wondering." She flipped a few pages. "Ew! Look at this bug!" Milo reached for his book, but Addy had already turned around and called out, "Noah! Zoe! Come and see this!"

Javi looked from Addy to Milo, confused. To his horror, Milo saw Noah and a girl with long braids and a basketball come walking over. Milo's plan was coming apart. He was becoming the center of attention.

Addy showed the kids his guide. Milo stared at the table. His hands were in tight fists. Any second, they would start teasing him. He'd heard it all before. *Geek. Nerd. Bug-Boy. Cripple.* He wanted to sink into the ground.

"Wow," Noah said. "These are so *real*."

"I know," said Addy. "Hey, that's this tree!"

The girl named Zoe turned to Milo. "You drew these? Is it all stuff you found around here?" Milo looked up. These kids weren't making fun of him. They were impressed.

Milo was surprised. He couldn't think of what to say.

Javi jumped in to help Milo. He had caught up with the conversation. "Milo draw this," he insisted. He pointed to the open page. "Dan-dee-lions everywhere!" Then he turned red. He was embarrassed that he had spoken to so many people at once.

Zoe laughed. Noah said, "Cool!" They sat down. Conversation started to drift to other topics. Addy was telling them about her broken leg. She was including all the gross details. Milo's heartbeat started to slow down. Their attention was no longer on him. He took back his guide. Javi smiled at him, shrugged, and put his headphones back on. Their corner was not going to be so quiet anymore.

But maybe, just maybe, that was going to be okay.

Chapter Five
The Speed Demon

Addy sat at the picnic table every day. She tutored Javi and chatted with Milo. Other kids came over to talk to Addy. She had been coming to The Club since she started school. She was friends with everybody. Milo thought Miguel looked pleased when he saw the knot of kids gathered under the tree.

But Milo still didn't join in much. It was one thing to nod and say hello to someone who came over to his table. It was another to draw attention to himself. To see people staring at his legs. To answer stupid questions. To wonder if they were being nice to him because of his crutches. Or to learn that they were making fun of him behind his back. Those were the kinds of things that had happened to him before.

Not that Milo expected that from Addy. She could talk your ear off, but she was really friendly. She was interested in everything. She got Javi to show her his cassette tapes. Milo thought this was smart. Addy got Javi to speak English by asking him about the music.

And she enjoyed science. Addy said she wanted to be a doctor. "I might as well," she added, "since I've spent half my life in emergency rooms." She insisted on reading Milo's whole field guide. Her favorite page was the red oak. She loved the story about the seedling and the fence. Just like Milo.

It was late September, and the tree was dropping its new crop of acorns. The nuts kept bouncing across the table or off their heads. The squirrels chased after them and buried them all over the yard. It was fun to watch. Every day when they arrived, they had to sweep acorns off the table before they sat down.

"How many acorns can a tree drop anyway?" said Addy, as she fished three or four out of Javi's hoodie.

"About 10,000 on a big tree like this," said Milo. He had been reading up on oaks for his guide. "But most of them get eaten or fall where they can't sprout. Only a few ever get a chance

to grow." Addy started making up crazy stories about a superhero acorn. The acorn fought off evil squirrels and fences in order to survive. Milo laughed more than he had in a long time.

The next week, Milo arrived to find the The Club's outdoor space transformed. Folding tables had been set up. There were tools piled all over them. There was a stack of lumber leaning against a wall. There were bins of safety glasses, wheels, bolts, cables, paint…

Everything a team would need to build their go-kart.

Milo, Javi, and Addy watched from their table as the middle school kids at The Club gathered in the yard. Miguel got everyone organized. "Is everyone here? You should be standing with your team. Each team should have three kids." There was some shifting and talking as kids found each other.

Miguel continued. "You have four days to design and build your go-kart. There are a few parent volunteers around to help. But we want you to do as much as you can on your own. The rally is on Friday. Each team will do three runs down the course. We have a few prizes. Fastest go-kart, best-designed go-kart, and coolest-looking go-kart. But the main thing is to have fun. Let's get started!"

Teams gathered around their tables. There was lots of talking and laughing. Adults wandered from team to team. They showed kids how to use the tools. They gave tips and suggestions for designs.

Milo, Javi, and Addy tried to focus on their normal work. But it was all pretty distracting. People were having a lot of fun.

Addy put down the book she was reading. She sighed. "I've done the go-kart rally ever since I was old enough to sign up. It's weird to be watching this year."

She paused. Then she added, "Of course, last year I crashed into another go-kart and broke my arm. And the year before that I cut a picnic table in half with a saw. It was an accident. But Miguel was pretty mad."

Javi was puzzled. "Happy memory?" he said.

Addy laughed. "Yeah! Happy memory." She pulled out her phone. "This is a picture of last year's 'kart. Before I crashed it, of course. We called it *The Speed Demon*. Zoe and Noah were on my team. They had to split up and find other teams this year because of my leg." She sounded a little sad.

Milo looked at the photo. Addy stood with Noah and Zoe next to an electric blue go-kart. It had a red fire demon painted on the side. *Noah probably did that*, Milo thought. He really was a good artist. The go-kart was sleek, cool, and fast. It was beautiful. To Milo, it was love at first sight.

Milo had been born with his disability. The doctors weren't sure at first if he would ever walk. It had taken him a long time. After years of physical therapy, his movements were still jerky, awkward, and slow. He had never biked or skied or skateboarded. Every move he made had to be done carefully and slowly. He tried to imagine driving *The Speed Demon*. How would it feel to speed smoothly down a hill without braces or crutches?

Milo was distracted on the ride home. When his mom asked him questions, he answered absently. He was thinking about the go-kart. He thought about it through dinner. He thought about it as he lay in bed. For a whole month, Milo had refused to sign up for anything at The Club. Now he'd found something he really wanted to try. But it was the one thing he couldn't do.

Or was it?

Milo had an idea.

Chapter Six
A New Idea

Milo arrived at the picnic table the next day. He was still thinking about his idea. He looked across the yard. It was full of activity. Most teams had completed their designs. They were starting to build. The air was filled with the sounds of saws, drills, and hammers. Zoe was gluing two pieces of wood together. Noah was making some kind of tail fin.

Milo turned around. Addy was listening to

Javi read an assignment aloud in English. Suddenly, Milo interrupted. "Is there a rule," he asked Addy, "that you have to steer the go-kart with your feet?"

"Um, no," Addy said. "I guess there isn't. That's just the way they're always built. It keeps it simple…" Addy stopped. Her face changed. She had gotten the idea, too.

"What if we built one that we could steer with our hands?" Milo continued. Javi looked up. "Javi," Milo said. "You wouldn't mind being on our team, would you? You'd help us build a kart?"

Javi broke into a grin. He nodded. "I am building," he said. Milo wasn't sure what that meant, but he said, "Great!"

Addy said, "We'd better check if it's allowed." She spotted Miguel at Noah's table. "Miguel!" she called.

He came over. "What's up, guys?"

Addy told them their idea. Miguel thought

a minute. "You'd have to design a completely different front end," he said. "You and Milo can't put your feet on the axle to steer. It will be harder, but not impossible."

He looked at the three of them. "And it's not going to be easy for two of you to move around and get stuff."

Javi spoke up. "I will do that!"

Miguel broke into a big smile. "Cool!" he said. "Start making your plan!"

They worked all that afternoon. Addy was great at design. She said the kart should sit higher. It would be easier to get in. But it also needed to be wider. And have bigger wheels. That would make it stable.

Javi realized they needed to measure Milo's and Addy's legs. There had to be enough space on the kart's platform to brace them comfortably and securely. He was good at using the measurements to make a plan.

Milo drew all their ideas. His field guide work had given him plenty of practice. He could draw anything from different angles and to scale.

Miguel helped them figure out a simple steering wheel system. He promised to bring the extra parts they would need the next day. Milo suspected Miguel was breaking a few Club go-kart traditions to make their design happen. But he was also sure Miguel would do just about anything to get them to join in a Club activity. Miguel liked people to be involved.

By the end of the day, they had a working plan. They were excited as they packed up. They were really going to do this!

Zoe and Noah came over to see them. They were excited, too. Their go-karts were coming together. Noah's team was going for speed. His go-kart was low and long, to reduce drag. Zoe's team was more interested in style. They were building an old-fashioned-style 'kart with lots of cool woodwork. She was having fun learning to use a saw.

Addy said, "We're building a go-kart, too. We just started today." Noah and Zoe were surprised. Addy showed them the design. "It's super cool," said Noah finally. "But it's a ton of work. Do you think you can get it done in time?"

Milo looked around. People were taking tools inside and covering their work up for the night. Most teams had already cut out the boards for their karts. Some had even begun to put them together. There were only two more days. *Could* they finish in time?

Milo remembered what Miguel had said. "Hard, but not impossible." He smiled. It was like the little acorn that grew into the oak tree.

"We'll find a way," he said.

He hoped that was true.

Chapter Seven
Kart Crazy

It was Javi who got things going the next day. Milo was good at drawing and design. But he had never built anything. Addy had been on go-kart teams before. But she hadn't done much actual construction. She'd always been given the planning and painting jobs. Especially after she cut the picnic table in half.

But it turned out that when Javi said, "I am building," it meant, "I know how to use power tools."

And he did. He brought boards and plywood over to the table. He got Addy and Milo to measure and mark the wood. Soon, he was cutting lengths of lumber. Addy and Milo labeled each one. They laid them out on the picnic table. Then they drilled the pieces together. Addy only attached the frame to the table once. Milo thought everything was going pretty smoothly.

Kids came over from time to time to see what they were doing. Word had spread that their team was building something unusual. Everyone said nice things. But Milo knew they had to be wondering if his team could succeed.

He got it. Their team was one kid who barely spoke English and two people on crutches. One of those two could barely walk in a straight line on a good day. The other was so famous for causing disaster that she was called Hurricane Addy. Their go-kart was more complicated than anyone else's. Oh, yeah, and they had started a day late.

Harder, Milo repeated to himself as he lined up a new piece of wood. *It's harder, but not impossible.*

His mom appeared out of nowhere. "Hey, Sport," she said. "I was wondering where you were. It's time to go home."

Milo blinked. The two hours he spent at The Club had never gone faster.

Milo gazed across the yard. There were

nearly finished go-karts everywhere. Most people only had painting left to do tomorrow.

"This looks great!" said his mom. She smiled at his teammates and introduced herself. He knew how glad she was to see him hanging out with other kids.

Milo stared at his team's go-kart. They had worked so hard. Everything was cut out. But it did not look great to him. The frame was only half put together. They had to put in the steering. And get the wheels on. Never mind the painting.

He wished he didn't have to leave.

In the car, his mom asked why he looked so worried. He told her that he thought they might run out of time. "The important thing is that you are trying new things," she said. "Don't worry so much about the finished product."

It was a mom kind of thing to say. Milo didn't think he could make her understand. He had been hurt badly by other kids in the past. He had spent a long time keeping to himself. Not trying anything that might risk failing in front of others. Now he had made a couple of friends. They were all knocking themselves out to build this kart. He thought everyone at The Club was watching to see if they could do it. It was a test. A test of whether he could belong to that world. Just like anyone else. If he couldn't…well, if he couldn't, it would be what he thought most people expected.

The next day, Milo and Addy got back to work on the frame. Milo could hear Addy muttering to herself, "Careful. Careful. Don't mess up." Milo was working on the wheels. He was thinking the same thing himself. They didn't have time for mistakes. Meanwhile, Javi and Miguel put together the steering. Everyone worked at top speed. But time was slipping away. A half an hour, and then an hour, was gone before they knew it. *We're never going to make it*, Milo thought.

"Hey, guys," said a voice behind them. "We came over to see if you needed any help." It was Noah. Zoe was right behind him.

"Yeah," Zoe said. "Our 'karts are done. The paint is drying."

Addy said, "You guys are the best! Thank you!"

Noah picked up a sander. Zoe got a power drill. They started to work faster. Things were coming together.

Milo sat down for a moment to rest. It took a lot of energy to stand and brace himself against the table so he could work. His legs were tired. He looked at all the people gathered around the go-kart. A month ago, he was determined not to meet anyone at The Club. Last night, he thought he had two friends. Now he had four. They were all talking and laughing around him. He was just another member of the team. An acorn dropped and bounced off his head. He smiled. He was finding his bit of sunlight.

Club was nearly over when they finished. They lifted the go-kart off the table. Javi rolled it back and forth. He tested the steering wheel. "Working!" he said. He had a huge smile on his face. Addy was excited, too. She was pointing out the 'kart's special features to a couple of friends.

Milo knew how his teammates felt. He couldn't take his eyes off the 'kart. It was beautiful. He turned to Zoe and Noah. "Thanks," he said. "We couldn't have done it without you."

"Too bad we couldn't get it painted," said Noah.

"What are you going to call it?" asked Zoe.

Addy laughed. "We haven't even talked about that. We were too busy."

"Well, think of something tonight," said Noah. "If I get a chance I'll paint it on tomorrow."

"Can we take a test run?" asked Milo. He was dying to try it out.

"Not now," said Miguel. "It's pick-up time. You need to clean up and get out of here. Don't forget to bring your helmets tomorrow."

When he got in the car, his mom said, as usual, "How did your day go?"

"Great!" Milo answered. And this time, he meant it.

Chapter Eight
The Rally

Friday was a bright blue, blazing orange kind of autumn day. The perfect weather, Milo thought. He couldn't wait to get to The Club. He couldn't wait to make a run down the hill in the go-kart. It was going to be the best day ever.

Miguel got a park worker to let them borrow a motorized cart. He drove Milo and Addy up the hill they used for the rally. A table had been set up like a racetrack pit area. It had tools and extra supplies for repairs. There were lots of parents

and siblings standing around. They were ready to
watch the event. Milo's mom and dad were there
with a camera.

Milo waved and
grabbed his helmet. He got
out of the cart and stood
at the edge of the hill.
It was wonderful to be
above the city. To feel
the space and light open
up around him. Milo wished he could come here
more often.

The hill was a grassy slope. It ended in a
wide, flat run. It was not the sort of hill where you
could build up a huge amount of speed. Milo was
pretty sure that was why Miguel chose it. But you
could ride for a long time. It would be enough.
Enough to leave his crutches behind. Enough to
break free.

Addy pointed. "Here comes Javi." He was with a bunch of other kids, pushing their go-karts up the hill. Zoe's kart was a glossy black with red trim. Noah's team had mixed glitter into their paint so that their kart gleamed like a silver bullet. Milo knew their go-kart

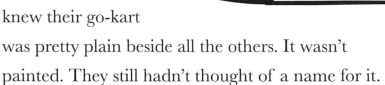

was pretty plain beside all the others. It wasn't painted. They still hadn't thought of a name for it. But Milo could not have been prouder.

Miguel got the teams organized. Only one go-kart would go down the hill at a time. Milo smiled. He thought Addy's crash last year might have had something to do with that. There were adults waiting at the bottom of the hill. They would measure each go-kart's speed and distance. Miguel went on about the prizes that would be given and how they would be decided. Milo didn't listen much. He didn't care about the prizes. He didn't expect to win any. He just wanted to make the run.

Finally, Miguel started sending go-karts down the hill. Zoe's and Noah's teams both went before Milo's. Their go-karts bumped down the hill without a hitch. Addy and Javi thought Milo should take their first run. He was the one who had pulled the team together in the first place. Their design had sprung from his idea. Milo gripped his helmet tightly and waited for his turn.

When Miguel called their team, Zoe and Noah started cheering. His parents started cheering. The whole crowd started cheering. Milo wanted to cheer with them. *See*! he wanted to say to them. *We did it*!

Javi pushed the go-kart into place and put on the brake. He held Milo's crutches while Miguel helped Milo get settled in the seat. The kart fit him perfectly. His legs were braced securely against a block. The steering wheel was in the exact right place. Milo put on his helmet. Miguel said, "You ready for this, man?"

Milo grinned. "I was born ready."

Miguel laughed. "Okay, then. Release the brake. Javi, on the count of three, give him one good push. One…two…three!"

Javi pushed. The crowd got even louder.
The go-kart dipped over
the edge of the
hill. It started
to gain speed.
Milo
shouted for the
pure joy of it.
For a moment,
he was flying.

Just for a moment.

The kart started to rattle. Then it started to wobble. Milo looked around, panicked. He didn't think the kart was supposed to do this. Suddenly, there was a bang, and the kart spun hard to one side. Milo was thrown out onto the ground.

The crowd went suddenly silent. Milo lay sprawled in the grass. He couldn't believe what had happened. He'd wiped out in front of everyone. *In front of everyone.*

It felt like the end of the world.

Chapter Nine
The End of the World

Milo struggled to sit up. The go-kart lay beside him. It was tipped at an awkward angle. The right front wheel was missing. It had come off while the kart was barreling down the hill. A bolt must have come loose. *That was my fault,* he thought. *I put on the wheels.*

He pulled

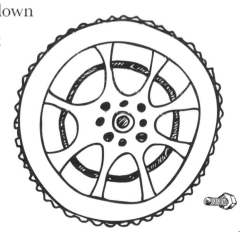

off his helmet. He'd had the wind knocked out of him. He wasn't hurt. But his eyes were stinging with tears. Now Miguel was running down the hill. His parents and Javi were close behind him.

"I'm okay," he said quickly as they reached him. "I'm okay." *Please, please don't make a scene*, he thought. The eyes of the whole crowd were on him. He tried to hold it together.

His father helped him to his feet. There was scattered clapping from the crowd. *Look away*, he thought angrily. *Don't look at me.*

"Are you really all right?" his mom said. Her eyes were worried. "*Yes*," Milo snapped. "I'm *fine*. Just please get me out of here!" He hated being this helpless. He couldn't do anything himself. He didn't have his crutches.

Miguel came up. "I can carry him back up the hill."

"NO!" Milo almost shouted.

"Take it easy, Milo," his father said. He was gripping Milo's shoulder. He understood. He said to Miguel, "Would you mind driving your cart down here? Then he can ride back up."

Miguel left. His dad turned back to him. "It's okay, Milo. It's all going to be okay."

Milo looked over at the go-kart. Javi was bending over it, checking the damage. *It's not okay*, thought Milo. *It's not okay at all.*

The next five minutes were the longest ones of Milo's life. He was the center of the crowd's attention as he waited for Miguel. He had to drive right past them when Miguel brought him back to the top of the hill. Some of them called out, "That's okay, kid!" or "You'll get it next time!" They were just being nice. Milo thought he knew what they were really thinking. *What else could you expect from someone like him? What were they thinking to let him drive a go-kart?*

Miguel seemed to know he needed space. He parked the cart away from the crowd under a big tree. He said quietly, "Don't let this get you down." Milo didn't respond.

Miguel sighed. "I've got to get back to the rally, Milo. You can sit here as long as you want." He walked away. Soon, Milo could hear the crowd cheering again. Another team must have made a run down the hill. It was all going on without him.

Milo's dad had gone to get their car. His mom was gathering his stuff. He was only waiting until they came back. The city surrounded the hill like a cage. He wanted to run away.

He heard Addy before he saw her. The familiar clunk of crutches gave her away. "Hey, Milo," she said. He didn't say anything. She climbed up beside him in the cart. Milo turned away angrily. *Doesn't she see that I want to be alone?*

"I don't think much of your crash," Addy

said lightly. "Mine was way more embarrassing. They didn't call an ambulance for you."

Milo's face was stony. *You can't make me laugh about this*, he thought. *It's not the same thing. Don't pretend it was the same.*

"You didn't even bust the go-kart. Noah, Zoe, and Javi brought it back up the hill. The wheel just needs to be put back on. They're fixing it now. It will probably be ready for the next run."

Milo kept staring ahead. *This was the problem with Addy*, he thought. *She never knew when to stop talking.*

She continued, "Miguel even says we can repeat our first run. He says everyone gets one do-over for technical failure."

That pushed Milo over the edge. "Technical

failure?" he snarled. "You mean *my* failure. *I* blew it. I didn't get that wheel on right the first time. I wiped out in front of that whole crowd. And it was my fault!" All his anger was pouring out now.

"I had to lie there, looking ridiculous, until someone helped me up. Everyone was watching. Everyone was whispering. 'That poor little handicapped kid. Too bad he couldn't pull it off!'" He turned and finally met her eyes. "And if you think I should go back over there so that all those people can talk about how brave the crippled boy is, you're crazy!"

Addy's face was red. Milo could see that she was angry, too. But she didn't yell. Instead, her voice was dangerously quiet. "That's not what I thought at all, Milo. I thought you should go back over there because we need you. I thought you should go back because you are part of our team!"

She grabbed her crutches, got out of the

cart, and stalked away. Well, as much as one could stalk away on crutches.

Milo sat in stormy silence as her words sank in. *What does she know?*

A breeze stirred. An acorn dropped from a branch above him and bounced off his head.

He glared up at the tree. "And you be quiet!" he muttered.

Chapter Ten
Flight of the Acorn

There is no way to sneak anywhere when you are on crutches, Milo thought. He wondered if this was the thing that he hated the most about them. They attracted attention. *Thunk, thunk* they went as he made his way back over to the edge of the hill.

Milo ran a hand through his hair and tried to straighten his back. *If you're going to make a spectacle of yourself, he thought, at least try to look good doing it.*

Heads turned as he edged his way through

the crowd. *People are always going to stare*, he thought. *That's just how it is.* He tried to shut his mind to them.

It was hard. Hard, but not impossible. He searched for his team.

Milo found Addy, Javi, and Zoe standing in a circle around the go-kart. The wheel was back on. They were watching Noah. He was bending over, working on something.

Noah stood up and said, "Done," as Milo reached them.

"Hey, guys," Milo said. They all turned around. He tried to sound super casual. "What's going on?"

Javi stepped forward. He pointed at the kart. "Milo! See! We have good name." He paused when he saw Milo's face. "You are okay?"

Milo looked. There was something painted on the front of the go-kart. Something with a

THE FLYING ACORN

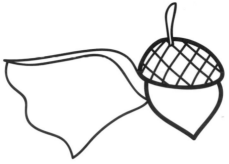

superhero cape spreading out behind it. Big letters arched over the picture. They said, "The Flying Acorn."

Milo smiled. "I'm great, Javi."

He stepped into the circle. "So, when's the next run?" This wasn't the end of his story.

Want to Keep Reading?

Turn the page for a sneak peek at
the next book in the series.

ISBN: 9781538382455

Chapter One
November

Javi slipped and slid on the icy path. Freezing water seeped into his thin sneakers. He shivered. *Maybe I should stop walking through the park.*

It was November. For two months, Javi had gotten off the city bus one stop early. He liked cutting through the park to his after-school program. There were tall, leafy trees and green meadows. They were a faint reminder of the colorful landscapes of his home.

But now, the park was empty. The sun was

already setting. The ground was covered in frost. Trees were brown and bare. A sharp wind found its way through his jacket. And Javi's hometown in the Guatemalan highlands seemed farther away than ever.

It had been four months since Javi had arrived in the United States with his mother, grandmother, and little sister. They were all living in his uncle's apartment. Javi and his sister were in school full-time. They had enough food to eat. What remained of his family was safe. Javi knew he should be grateful. But this new city was like a different planet. Who knew a park could be so silent, cold, and colorless?

Javi pulled his headphones out of his bag. He put them on carefully. He needed them to last. They were held together with tape in a couple of places.

He was even more careful with his cassette

player. It was tucked safely in an inner pocket. No amount of money could replace it. Nobody sold them anymore. And anyway, Javi didn't want anything new. This cassette player had belonged to his father.

Javi pressed the play button. The music washed over him. He remembered the last time he'd heard this song with Papá. They had sat close. They had each held an ear to a headphone.

They were trying to listen together.

Now, Papá was gone.

Javi didn't want to think about that.

He turned up the volume.

His father had loved American musicals. This song was from one of them. Javi hadn't understood the English words. Papá had tried to explain the story. It was about a poor family living in a cold place like this one. It had a funny name. *Fiddler on the Roof.* Javi loved the music. It was full of loss and longing. It seemed to fit his mood.

Javi's family used to spend many evenings singing songs from Papá's musicals. Or learning Guatemalan songs and legends from Javi's grandmother, Abuelita. Tevye and Maria von Trapp were familiar friends from the musicals. So was the Mayan hero Tecún Umán. And the quetzal. Javi loved folktales about the rare bird with shimmering green and red feathers. It lived in the cloud forests near their home.

The life Javi and his family had left behind hadn't been easy. But it had been full of music and stories.

ABOUT
the
AUTHOR

Elizabeth Gordon has a master's degree
in Children's Literature from Hollins
University. She was a finalist for the
Hunger Mountain Katherine Paterson
Prize for Young Adult and Children's
Writing, the winner of the Hollins
University Houghton Mifflin Harcourt
Scholarship, and winner of the SCBWI
Barbara Karlin Grant. She has published
nine middle grade books so far, including
a five-book superhero series.

the CLUB

Check out more books at:
www.west44books.com